THE ADVENTURES OF MOOLI AND THE BLUE-LEGGED ALIEN

Asha Nehemiah is a popular author with children of all age groups. Wonderfully funny characters get into hilarious adventures and crazy escapades in her stories. *Mystery of the Secret Hair Oil Formula*, *Mystery of the Silk Umbrella*, *Zigzag and Other Stories*, *Granny's Sari*, *The Rajah's Moustache* and *Trouble with Magic* are some of her published titles.

Her books have been translated into Hindi, Tamil, Bengali, Assamese and Urdu.

Published by Scholastic India Pvt. Ltd.
A subsidiary of Scholastic Inc., New York, 10012 (USA).
Publishers since 1920, with international operations in Canada, Australia, New Zealand, the United Kingdom, India, and Hong Kong.

For information regarding permission, write to:
Scholastic India Pvt. Ltd.
A-27, Ground Floor, Sigma Centre
Infocity-1, Sector 34, Gurgaon 122001 (India)

First edition: April 2017

ISBN-13: 978-93-5275-068-9

Reprinted by Scholastic India Pvt.Ltd., Sep.2017, Jan 2018, April, Feb. 202

Printed at Ram Printograph, Delhi.

The Adventures of Mooli and The Blue-Legged Alien

ASHA NEHEMIAH

Illustrations by Tanaya Vyas

SCHOLASTIC
New York Toronto London Auckland
Sydney New Delhi Hong Kong

Contents

Meddling Mooli	7
Missing Whiskers	14
Idea Number 8	20
Mr Reddy	27
Success at Last!	32
Genius Dad	38
Puris for Dinner	42
The Blue-Legged Alien	50
The Flower Thief	57
A Prize on *Wayouts*	64

Meddling Mooli

The trouble with Mooli was that his fingers seemed to have a mind of their own. So even when he was watching cartoons on TV, his fingers would be pulling the beads off a cushion cover.

Or tearing the newspaper into a heap of tiny paper balls. Or tugging the flowers till the vase toppled onto the floor.

Just yesterday, he had stuck one of his shoes to the floor with Super Glue. It

happened by mistake when he was repairing his remote-controlled toy aeroplane with Super Glue. Every day, Mooli's amma would have to tell him, 'Stop meddling, Mooli.'

One Friday morning, Mooli's family was very excited. Mooli's amma, who was a very good cook, was going to appear on a television cooking show. Amma sold home-made cakes and cookies. Her company was called "Yummy Scrummy Home-made Treats".

Amma had packed all the things she would take to the TV studio in a large cardboard box. She packed the butter, sugar

YUMMY
SCRUMMY
HOMEMADE
TREATS

and even the little bottles of food colouring. Then, she taped the lid shut with sticky tape. She wanted to make sure that Mooli didn't meddle with the things kept in the box.

Mooli was excited too—but for a different reason. He was busy collecting things for a project of his own. He was the first to eat his breakfast that morning. Then, checking that his parents were nowhere in sight, he quickly put a packet of balloons into his backpack, followed by a pair of scissors. Then, in went this, that, and the other—all things that he was not supposed to meddle with. Soon, his backpack was quite heavy. But it didn't matter. This time, Mooli was making sure that he and his friend Soups would win a prize on *Wayouts*.

Supriya George (Soups) and Murali

Krishnan (Mooli) had been friends since they were babies. Their mothers were best friends. Though Soups and Mooli went to different schools, they met on most days after school.

It was Supriya's dad, Uncle George, who had shown the children a very cool new website called *Wayouts*. It stood for "**W**orld's **A**s **Y**et **O**riginal **U**ntried **T**ricks and **S**tunts". *Wayouts* was something like a book of world records, but different in some important ways. *Wayouts* was a website. It had to be read on the computer and not on paper. The winners didn't have to do something faster or better than others. They simply had to do things that had never been tried before. Something that was, yes, Original and Untried.

WAYOUTS
World's As Yet Original Untried Tricks and Stunts
1st PRIZE
Chingo Grogovitch for painting a picture with his toes while standing on his head
2nd PRIZE
Lalchand Chopra for frying 73 jalebis with his left hand while making 40 samosas with his right hand

This is what a page from *Wayouts* looked like.

WINNERS IN JULY

First prize: Chingo Grogovitch for painting a picture with his toes while standing on his head.

Second prize: Lalchand Chopra for frying 73 jalebis with his left hand while making 40 samosas with his right hand.

'I'm off to school. Bye!' Mooli called out as he left home to catch his school bus. 'Oops!' he said, as his backpack knocked down a pile of books and papers from the table. Then, looking at the object in his hand, he added, 'I wonder how this magnet came into my hands.'

Missing Whiskers

'I wonder why Mooli was in such a hurry,' said Amma.

She was ready to leave for the TV studio where she would be filmed making her special Coconut-Frosted Almond Cookies.

'Where is my list? I fixed it to the refrigerator with a magnet.' Amma looked around.

She picked up the box. The top was still taped firmly shut. 'Wasn't it very clever of me to tape up ... *erk* ...' Amma stopped

suddenly. She looked puzzled. The box was in her hands, but all the things she had packed in it were lying on the floor. The butter was lying in a pool of broken eggs. The flour was mixed with pink food colouring.

The flaps at the bottom of the box were open. All the things she had packed had fallen out of the bottom. 'Could it have been Mooli?' she thought.

'Here's your list, Gita,' said Appa, holding out a piece of paper. 'But wait, what's this written behind the list?'

Amma turned the list around to read what Mooli had scribbled at the back:

I have taken your whiskers. I will return them after we finish our stunt for Wayouts.

'What does Mooli mean? I don't have whiskers. You don't have whiskers either, Ravi,' she told Mooli's appa. 'I wish Supriya's dad hadn't got the children interested in *Wayouts*. It's been nothing but trouble all around since they decided they must win a prize on *Wayouts*.'

'True. Nothing but tricks and stunts by them. Leading to trouble and problems for us. They've tried new things seven times during the summer holidays. And failed each time. I hope they'll give up the idea soon,' said Appa.

Amma started putting all the things back

into the box. She put in fresh eggs and more flour. 'Where is my electric beater? I need it to beat the eggs, sugar and butter.'

'Aah ha ...' said Appa, with a knowing look. 'I think you are searching for your whiskers, Gita. I think Mooli has taken your elcctric beater. Only, he calls it "whiskers" in his note. Because it whisks things!'

'Mooli! How could he? Why can't he stop meddling?'

Amma looked very annoyed indeed. True, she could use a regular hand-beater. But that would be so much more difficult. And also take more time. Suddenly, she spotted one of Mooli's favourite toys lying on the dining table. She picked it up. She looked at it for a moment and then put it into her box.

Idea Number 8

When Soups and Mooli first decided that they would win a prize on *Wayouts*, they had made lists of all the tricks and stunts they could try.

Supriya's list:

1) Stand on my left foot and write a poem that reads the same backwards and forwards.

2) Stand on my right foot and ... (there was a lot of stuff scratched out after that).

Mooli's list ran to four pages of ideas. Written in a small handwriting. On both sides

of the paper and filling all the margins too.

Soups had to agree that Mooli's ideas were better than hers. Yesterday, they had tried Idea no. 8. It hadn't worked well, but they were going to try again today. Idea no. 8 went like this: Mooli would have a scarf tied over his eyes. Then he would shoot an arrow onto a globe. The arrow was supposed to land on a particular country on the globe. To make things more difficult, the name of the country would be called out just as the globe was set spinning.

Soups and Mooli had a globe and a toy bow. They also had toy arrows. The kind which had small suction cups at one end instead of a pointed tip.

When they had tried the stunt yesterday, not even a single arrow had touched the globe.

To make things worse, they lost three of their four arrows. One hit Mrs Mehta's dog. One landed in the balcony of a flat where no one lived. The third one got trapped in the branches of a tall tree.

'That's why I brought this packet of balloons today,' Mooli explained.

'Look how I've cut the balloons into ribbons. See how stretchy each bit is.' Mooli stretched the piece he'd cut. Then, he tied the pieces together to make a long bit of stretchy string. Finally, he tied the stretchy bit of string to their last arrow. 'Now, it's simple to pull the arrow back from wherever it lands. We won't lose it. We can try our stunt even a hundred times till we get it right.'

'What's this electric beater for?' Soups asked.

'That's for the next idea. Idea no. 9. That's what we'll try if this stunt doesn't work,' Mooli said.

Once they collected all the things they needed, there was one very important job left.

They had to get Supriya's dad. In order to enter their trick on *Wayouts*, the children had to send in a picture or a video of the stunt. They could also send a letter from a person who had seen the stunt being performed.

Mr George, Supriya's dad, worked mainly from home. He was some sort of a genius who wrote the programmes which made computers do all sorts of amazing things. There was a note stuck on his door which said: *Do not disturb. Do not knock. Do not call me unless a Grizzly Bear has got into the house.*

So Soups didn't disturb or knock or call.

Instead, she made three glasses of mango milkshake using the electric mixer. The mixer whirred loudly. Within seconds, the door of Mr George's office room opened.

'I hope there's mango milkshake for me?' he asked. He headed straight for the sofa in front of the TV.

'Dad, since you're taking a break, could

you please bring your video camera out onto the balcony? Could you take a video of our stunt for *Wayouts*?' Supriya asked.

'Sure,' nodded her dad, sipping his milkshake. His eyes never left the TV screen.

Mr Reddy

Soups and Mooli chose a good spot to set up the globe. A place where no children played and no dogs were walked. The scarf was tied around Mooli's eyes. He held the bow and arrow in position. Soups spun the globe. It made a clicking sound as it whirled.

As Mooli took aim, Soups shouted out, 'Azerbaijan!'

The arrow went flying. There was a nice loud thunk.

'Yipee,' thought Mooli, 'the arrow has hit something.' He tore the silk scarf off his eyes in excitement, only to find Mr Reddy towering over him. The arrow was stuck to the middle of Mr Reddy's forehead!

Mr Reddy lived in Khushi Apartments where Supriya and her family also lived. He was in charge of the beautiful gardens there. Every morning, he would go around checking that the flowers had been watered and the weeds had been pulled.

'You naughty children! I've caught you both.' He sounded so angry that sparks seemed to fly out of the tips of his long moustache. 'So it's the two of you who have been shooting and stealing my flowers. My beautiful giant zinnias that I've been growing for the Best Garden Competition.'

Soups looked up at the balcony where her dad had been filming them on his video camera. Her dad waved cheerfully. He gave Soups a double thumbs-up sign and then went back inside the house. 'Oh no! Dad thinks our stunt was to shoot Mr Reddy in the middle of his forehead!'

'Please, Mr Reddy,' Supriya pleaded. 'We haven't stolen your giant flowers.'

'It couldn't be anyone else. This bit of the garden is fenced. This gate is kept locked.

No one can get near the flowers. How did the flowers vanish then? The two of you must have shot the flowers from that side of the fence. Then, you would have used this string to pull the flowers to yourself.'

The arrow now dangled from the string that Mr Reddy was holding.

'Perhaps it was aliens.' Mooli could think of no other explanation for the stolen flowers. 'You know those creatures from outer space.'

'There is no way my friend Murali could have shot the flowers,' Soups explained. 'He's missed everything he's aimed for so far. Let me show you.'

The two decided that they would do the stunt again. Just to show Mr Reddy that Mooli could never shoot straight.

Supriya tied the silk scarf over Mooli's eyes. She twirled the globe faster than ever.

'Mozambique,' she shouted out.

Mooli's arrow left the bow. But this time, it flew straight and true. The arrow hit the globe with a loud thunk and stuck to it.

Mr Reddy walked to the globe and picked up the arrow. One finger pointed to the spot where the arrow had just been stuck.

'Mozambique!' he read out, looking at them very suspiciously. Now, he was absolutely sure that Soups and Mooli had stolen his flowers.

Success at Last!

'Yippeee! We did it! We completed the stunt! We're going to win a prize on *Wayouts*!' Soups jumped up and down so happily that the sparkly hairband, holding her curly hair in place, fell onto the grass.

'I hope your Dad was watching us,' Mooli looked up. The balcony of the Georges' home was empty.

'Oh no! Dad went inside some time ago. He did not take a video of us doing our

stunt. He wasn't watching us either. If only there was some other person who saw us doing our stunt!' Soups thought aloud.

Both their eyes turned to Mr Reddy.

Soups went up to him and explained how Mooli and she wanted to win a prize on *Wayouts*. 'And now that we've actually completed a stunt successfully, we stand a very good chance. Please could you write a letter saying that you saw us doing the stunt?'

'You want me to certify that the two children who shot my prize-winning flowers have done something good? Absolutely not.' Mr Reddy turned around to walk away.

'Wait, please,' Soups called out. 'How about if we agreed to guard your giant flowers night and day? So that no one can steal any more flowers. So that the garden looks lovely on the day of the Garden Competition. Would you agree then, to write that you saw us do the stunt?'

'You keep my flowers safe first. I'll think about it later,' said Mr Reddy as he walked away. For days, he'd been dreaming about the garden at Khushi Apartments winning a prize at the Best Garden Competition.

'Are you crazy, Soups?' Mooli asked when Mr Reddy had left. 'How can we guard the flowers? I don't even live here. I suggest we forget all about this stunt. Mr Reddy is never going to write the letter for us. Let's go on to Idea no. 9. That's "Whisk a Sculpture". The one where we take the electric beater and some modelling clay ...'

'Stop, Mooli. Stop right there,' Soups said firmly. 'Don't be so impatient. I *am* going to

get the letter from Mr Reddy. And we *are* going to enter our stunt on *Wayouts*.'

'Fine,' Mooli agreed, 'but I wonder who would even want to steal these flowers.

They're pink! And purple! And I want to know how we're supposed to guard these flowers.'

'Hello!' Soups smiled, 'I have a father who is a genius.'

Genius Dad

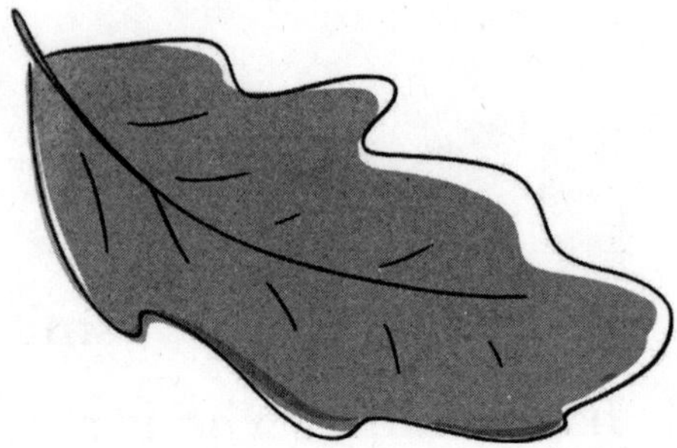

When the children saw Soups' dad at work, they realised why he was called a genius. The idea he came up with was brilliant.

He got Mr Reddy to let them into the garden. Then, he placed his video camera on its stand and put it behind a bush. He arranged the broad green leaves of the bush to hide the camera.

'This camera is going to watch those giant flowers day and night,' said Soups' dad. 'But

only when someone comes near it. I have put the camera on a motion-activated mode. Do you know what that means?'

He had to explain. 'It means that the camera comes on only when there is some movement in front of it. It gets switched on if a man or a woman walks in front of it ...'

'Or an alien,' Mooli cut in. He was sure that aliens were involved in this flower theft. Hadn't Mr Reddy said that there were no footprints anywhere near the flower beds? It had to be aliens.

'Right, so whenever someone comes near these flowers, the camera gets turned on and films everything. We will play it back and find out who the thief is. No person—or alien—' he added with wink at Mooli, 'can escape us.'

As they were about to leave the fenced area, Mooli stopped for a second. 'This leaf is hiding most of the camera,' he thought. He moved the leaf. He steadied the camera stand.

What Mooli didn't realise was that with all his meddling, the camera had moved slightly. Now, the camera was not focussed on the flowers. Instead, it was focussed on the blank white wall which was behind the flowers.

Puris for Dinner

Later that same evening, Mooli was back at home. He was eating dinner with his amma and appa.

'Isn't it wonderful how a day can start off so badly but then turn out well?' asked Mooli's amma with a wide smile. She had made Mooli's favourite dinner—puris with channa. The TV shoot had gone really well.

'Today, the cookies I made turned out better than any cookies I've ever made. They were delicious,' she said. 'Which was surprising, because someone had taken my electric beater. It's quite difficult to beat the sugar and butter without an electric beater.'

'I'm sorry, Amma,' Mooli said, 'I didn't know you needed the electric beater for the TV shoot.'

'Then there was Mrs Kirorimal,' Amma went on as though Mooli hadn't spoken. 'She had ordered a dinosaur-shaped birthday cake for her son's birthday party. I was supposed to send the cake along with a packet of dinosaur-shaped balloons and a packet of dinosaur-shaped candles. I sent everything she wanted. But the packet of balloons, that I sent along with the cake, had just vanished. I wonder where the balloons went.'

'For a walk in the dinosaur forest maybe?' Mooli grinned.

BALLOONS

'You can't blame Mooli for that, Gita,' said Appa. 'What use would he have for a packet of balloons?'

'I don't know. But honestly, ever since Soups and he decided to win a prize on *Wayouts*, Mooli has some use for everything. Whether it is a can opener or a measuring tape. Whether it's a fridge magnet or a pack of toothpicks. Once, he even took all my hair clips. And what about the time he took your shoe laces?' asked Amma.

Amma ran her fingers over Mooli's head. His straight, spiky hair felt like the bristles of a toothbrush.

'No more meddling with my things, Mooli. That's a promise, okay? Now hurry up and finish your dinner. Appa and I will clear the table.'

'Mmm ...' Mooli nodded, as his mouth was full. Eating puris always helped Mooli get lots of new ideas. He was thinking as he ate. He could hear his parents talking in the kitchen.

'I think that the children's interest in *Wayouts* hasn't been a bad thing altogether.' That was Amma.

'Well, it has certainly kept all of us busy over summer. I had to repaint the garage wall where Mooli and Soups were trying to paint "football pictures." That's what the stunt was called. They dipped a football in paint and kicked it onto the wall, trying to paint a picture on it. Yes, I was certainly kept busy.'

Appa did not add that the football had also crashed through their window and landed on their carpet. It had also bounced off his car. That had left a green dent on his silver car!

'Well, *Wayouts* has been good for Soups,' said Amma. 'George and Nirmala are happy that she's been spending more time outdoors. That girl spends too much time on her books.'

'True. Soups is happy only when she has

a book in hand. She's actually quite a good influence on Mooli,' added Appa.

'Well, if you ask me, I think Mooli is good

for her. He's showed her how books can be used to build a fort, or a car racing track, or to prop up a table with a broken leg!'

'The table leg that he broke in the first place ...' Appa and Amma came out of the kitchen laughing.

Amma hugged Mooli. 'This Mooli of mine has got so many ideas that if each idea was a little bubble of air, he would be bobbing up and down like a balloon. Right?'

'Right,' Mooli grinned and he actually bobbed his way to the kitchen to put away his plate.

The Blue-Legged Alien

It was Saturday morning. Supriya's flat was a five-minute walk from Mooli's house. When Mooli reached Khushi Apartments, he heard people talking loudly.

The loudest voice belonged to Mr Reddy. He was in the garden with Soups and some of their neighbours.

'One more of my giant zinnias has been stolen,' he was shouting. 'At this rate, there won't be a single flower left on any of the plants on the day of the Best Garden

Competition.' This time Mr Reddy was so angry that bolts of lightning seemed to flash from the tips of his moustache.

'Weren't you both supposed to guard my flowers?' Mr Reddy asked when he spotted Mooli.

'I am sure we've caught your thief this time. This is going to be the last time someone steals your flowers,' said Soups, picking up the video camera. Mooli picked up the stand and they both raced upstairs to Soups' flat.

Soups' mother was a doctor and had already left for work. Her dad was reading the newspaper. He was dressed for work in his mango-coloured kurta.

When they told him what had happened, Soup's dad attached the video camera to the TV. This way, they could watch the video on the TV screen.

The first time the camera came on was when a butterfly flew by. They could see the butterfly against the white wall.

A white wall in place of the giant zinnias? What was happening?

'Hey, what's this?' Soups' dad sounded very puzzled. 'Someone has moved the camera. It misses the flowers totally. What we can see now is a patch of blank wall that is about five feet above the flowers. I don't think the camera will catch the thief! Who could have meddled with the camera, I wonder!'

The look on Mooli's face gave him the answer to that question. Soups sighed. They would have to try a new stunt for *Wayouts*. Since they hadn't caught the flower thief, she didn't think that Mr Reddy would agree to write the letter to *Wayouts*.

Mooli and she were talking about what they'd try next when they heard a shout. Soups' dad had been watching the rest of the video to see if he could spot anything. And he had!

'Come here at once, kids,' Dad sounded very excited. 'Mooli, you were quite right about the aliens. Watch this.'

He rewound the video and played it again. First, there was only the blank white wall. Then, they noticed that something had entered the top right corner of the screen.

It was a foot. A blue foot! This was followed by a blue ankle. Then, a pair of blue legs in striped silk pajamas.

'So it was an alien, after all,' Mooli said in wonder, 'a blue-legged alien! But what are those strings?'

More of the blue-legged alien came into the frame. That was when they saw that it wasn't an alien, after all. It was a string puppet.

Someone was letting a puppet down

using the strings. The puppet seemed to grin wickedly as it went out of the frame.

The blue-legged puppet was missing from the frame for less than a minute. Then, it bobbed back into view. Someone was pulling it up. When it came back into the frame, the puppet had a beautiful flower in its hands. It was a giant-sized purple zinnia.

Soups' dad rewound the video again. He stopped at the frame of the puppet with a flower in its hands. 'That's your thief,' he said. 'Someone is letting the puppet down by its strings. They are using the puppet to steal the flowers.'

'The flower thief probably lives in the flat with the balcony just above the flower bed,' Soups worked out. 'It must be the first floor flat.'

1-D

The Flower Thief

Soups and Mooli rang the bell to Flat 1-D. As soon as the door opened, they spotted the thief. He was smiling wickedly at them from the wall.

On the wall inside the flat, was a fabulous collection of puppets. Puppets of all shapes and sizes. There, in between a glove puppet and an Indonesian shadow puppet was the puppet with blue legs and striped silk pyjamas.

‘Who are you looking for? What do you want?’ asked the boy who had opened the door. He was older than them.

‘We are looking for a blue-legged puppet,’ said Mooli.

‘I don’t know what you mean,’ stammered the boy, turning pale.

‘And we need to ask your puppet some questions. Like where it was between 5.47 am and 5.51 am this morning?’ Soups sounded like a detective. ‘That is the exact time shown on the video we have.’

This time the boy said, ‘Shh.’ He stepped out into the corridor and closed the door behind him.

Soups and Mooli told him that they had a video of the puppet stealing flowers. ‘We know that the flower thief lives in your flat.’

1-D

'The flowers were for my Science Teacher. She loves flowers,' said the boy. 'And she really loved those giant pink flowers. I didn't think anyone would mind. After all, there are new flowers growing on those plants all the time. Please don't tell anyone—especially Mr Reddy—what I did,' he pleaded.

'We won't tell anyone,' said Mooli, 'but only if you promise that you and your puppet won't steal any more flowers.'

The boy kept his promise. Both he and his blue-legged puppet left the flowers alone. New flowers bloomed every day and there were plenty of giant zinnias in the garden on the day of the Best Garden Competition.

The gardens at Khushi Apartments looked so wonderful that they won the First Prize.

Mr Reddy came to Soups' flat carrying the

big silver cup they had won. He also brought a letter with him.

It was the letter to *Wayouts* stating that he had seen Soups and Mooli doing their stunt.

'Now we can enter our stunt on *Wayouts*,' Mooli waved the letter happily.

'And this time we are sure to win the prize,' Soups added.

A Prize on *Wayouts*

One afternoon, about two weeks later, Soups and Mooli were sitting in front of the TV. There was a huge bowl of buttered popcorn next to them.

Normally, they were not allowed to watch TV on school days. But today was different. Mooli's amma was going to appear on TV. Soups' dad was making strawberry milkshake while the children waited for the show to start.

He felt the children needed to be cheered

up. Especially after the disappointing news that their stunt had not won a prize.

Soups' dad was the one who had helped the kids send their entry to *Wayouts*. He was the one who had got an email in reply.

The email said:

Dear Murali and Supriya,

Thank you for your entry to Wayouts *giving details of your stunt. We'd like to inform you that just three months ago, two ladies from Windygates, Scotland, completed the exact same stunt successfully. They won a prize for it.*

Please ask your parents, or any responsible adult, to help you read the winning entries on our website each month.

Thank you for your interest. Keep trying.

'I can't believe that two women, thousands of kilometres away, thought of the same

stunt as us,' said Mooli, munching on the popcorn.

'Yes, things can't get stranger than this,' Soups agreed.

She was wrong. What happened next was even stranger.

Amma's cooking show came on.

'Your amma looks really nice on the show. Really pretty,' said Soups.

On the screen, Amma was showing viewers how to make Coconut-Frosted Almond Cookies.

'The next step is to whisk the butter and sugar together till the mixture is soft and creamy,' said Amma from the TV screen.

'Normally, I use an electric beater. But today, I don't have my electric beater with me. You could even use a hand whisk or a

wooden spoon. Today, I'm going to use this instead.' She picked up a small black box.

'Hey!' said Mooli. 'That box looks like the remote of my toy aeroplane. Remember the one I repaired, Soups? The one with the propeller on its nose?'

Soups nodded.

The TV audience went "Aaah" as the

aeroplane flew over the bowl. Amma was guiding it with the remote.

Then, guided by Amma, the aeroplane dived into the bowl and the propellers whisked the sugar and butter.

'That's so cool,' laughed Mooli.

Soups clapped her hands as she watched. 'Your amma must be the first person in the world to make cookies using a remote-controlled toy,' she said.

'I'm sure no one has ever tried that before,' Mooli smiled.

Then, they stopped laughing and looked at each other. Both were thinking of the same thing.

"Your amma should be on *Wayouts*!' said Soups.

'Yes, of course,' Mooli smiled.

One month later, there she was ... on the *Wayouts* website.

Third Prize: Gita Krishnan for making cookies using a remote-controlled toy aeroplane.

FORTHCOMING

NEXT IN THE SERIES

The Adventures of Mooli and the Bully on Wheels

Mooli and Soups are still on their mission to win a prize on *Wayouts*. Their tricks and stunts get more creative than ever and they have a rollicking time. They create paintings from toothpaste, draw maps with spaghetti and meet a bully intent on stopping them.

Do Mooli and Soups manage to outwit the bully and finally win the prize?

OTHER BOOKS BY ASHA NEHEMIAH

The Mystery of the Secret Hair Oil Formula
Asha Nehemiah

An adventure story peopled with oddballs like a maniacal scientist and a sentimental wrestler.

ISBN: 9788176555654

The Mystery of the Silk Umbrella
Asha Nehemiah

A gorgeous silk umbrella brings mystery and mayhem into Arjun and Divya's lives.

ISBN: 9788184776904

Zigzag and Other Stories
Asha Nehemiah

A collection of 10 stories that will fill you with laughter, wonder and surprise.

ISBN: 9788184778274

The Boy Whose Nose Was Rose
AND MORE ROLLICKING STORIES
Asha Nehemiah

This collection of 12 wonderfully funny stories delights readers with its mix of warmth, wit, and fantasy.

ISBN: 9789351030027